BENVENUTO

Edmée, this is for you.

Weekly Reader Children's Book Club presents

Benvenuto

by
Seymour Reit

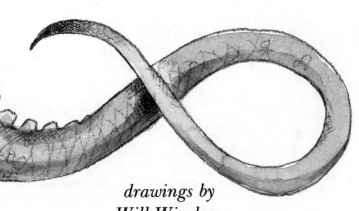

drawings by
Will Winslow

▲ Addison-Wesley

An Addisonian Press Book

Addison-Wesley Publishing Company, Inc.
Reading, Massachusetts 01867
Printed in the United States of America
First Printing

HA/HA   3/74   06297

Library of Congress Cataloging in Publication Data
Reit, Seymour.
  Benvenuto
  SUMMARY: Twelve-year-old Paolo brings back to
New York City an unusual and rare pet from camp—
a dragon.
  [1. Dragons—Fiction] I. Winslow, Will, illus.
II. Title.
PZ7.R2785Be   [Fic]   73-15625
ISBN 0-201-06297-6

CONTENTS

CHAPTER 1
ARRIVAL OF BENVENUTO

The kids who got off the bus, after two weeks at the Fresh Air camp, were all carrying more than when they had left. They piled out noisily, and with them came half the total wildlife of the Catskill Mountains.

There were straggly bouquets of wildflowers, huge bunches of wilting ferns, and plastic baggies filled with pine cones. There were snakes and tadpoles in jars. There were frogs and turtles in boxes. There were spiders and caterpillars in paper bags. There were swallowtail butterflies in old coffee containers. There was a

7

slightly stunned praying mantis in a covered jelly glass. And one girl clutched an enormous wasps' nest which, fortunately, the wasps had vacated.

Paolo, who was twelve years old, got off the bus last. He was lugging a cardboard carton tied with heavy twine and poked full of air holes. It was the biggest box of all.

The whole Bruno family had come to the bus station to welcome Paolo home.

"What's in the box?" squealed Gina, who was only nine and who had been to the same camp earlier that summer. "A raccoon? A skunk?"

"Shut up," Paolo replied.

"Talk nice to your sister," Mr. Bruno said.

Mrs. Bruno pointed to the carton. "That," she said, "goes back on the bus."

"You don't even know what it *is* yet," Paolo protested.

"A headache—that's what it is," said Mrs. Bruno grimly.

"I bet it's a rabbit," said Gina.

"Whatever it is, I don't like it," Mrs. Bruno continued.

"But, ma. Please—"

Mr. Bruno took a hand. "Everybody pipe down. The whole Port Authority building doesn't have to know our business. We'll hash it out when we get home."

He picked up Paolo's battered suitcase and herded the family out the Ninth Avenue exit and over to the corner bus stop.

The ride downtown to Bleecker Street was fairly peaceful, mostly because the bus was crowded and they all had to scatter to find seats. An uneasy truce continued while they climbed the three flights of stairs to their apartment. But once inside, they gathered expectantly around Paolo's precious carton.

"Okay, big game hunter," said Paolo's father, "let's have a look." Paolo knelt and carefully untied the twine. He slowly raised the lid. Everybody peeked inside.

"Icch," said Mrs. Bruno.

"That's some hell of a lizard," said Mr. Bruno.

"It's not a lizard!" Gina shrieked. "It's a baby dragon! A dragon! I have a drawing of one in my schoolbook!"

She flew into her room and came running back with the book. They stared at the drawing for a long time. Then at the strange scaly creature in the box. Mr. Bruno scratched his chin slowly. Of course there were no such things as dragons. He knew that. Everyone knew that. Dragons weren't real. They were strictly make-believe. Animals in fairy tales. And yet—Paolo's animal did look like the drawing in the book. In fact, *exactly* like the drawing. *Senza dubbio*—there was no doubt about it.

The little animal squinted up at Paolo devotedly. He put his stubby legs on the edge of the lid, tried to climb out, lost his balance and fell backward with a plop. His tail flapped feebly and a small wisp of blue smoke drifted from his nostrils.

Mr. Bruno shook his head. "A city apartment is no place to bring up a dragon," he said. "It isn't fair to him."

"Guess who'll wind up doing all the work," added Mrs. Bruno.

"You won't, ma," Paolo pleaded. "Honest. I'll take care of him all by myself. I *promise.*"

"That's what you said last year about the parakeets."

The dragon (for that's precisely what he was) untangled himself at last. He gazed up at the family with soulful eyes and belched softly. Paolo stared at him with a worried frown.

"He's been cooped up in there a pretty long time," he said. "I'd better take him downstairs and walk him."

Gina peered into the carton again.

"You're too late," she said.

Mrs. Bruno threw up her hands and paced around the room, muttering rapidly to herself in Italian. Paolo tagged after her.

"You don't understand," he said. "We were all on this hike in the woods, see? And we found him in this funny little cave. All alone. No mother. No father. *Nobody*. He looked half dead, like he was starving. I gave him a baloney sandwich, and then he began following me and following me. And sort of crying. I couldn't just *leave* him there like that. So I wrapped him up in my jacket and carried him back to camp."

"In your brand new jacket?"

"I took care of him the whole time I was away, for almost two weeks. I practically saved his whole entire *life*. He's used to me, ma. He *needs* me."

"Please, mama," said Gina, close to tears.

Mrs. Bruno turned to her husband. "What do you think, Salvatore?"

"I think my kid is a nut." He bent down, bringing his face close to Paolo's, and wagged a stubby finger. "Listen to me, big game hunter. You want a pet, you have to take the responsibility. *Responsabilita*. Understand? The first time you don't do your job—the first time your mother has to feed that animal, or walk him, or do anything *you're* supposed to do—"

"Yay! We can keep him!" Gina shouted. Paolo wasn't able to say a word. He just threw himself at his father and gave him a tight hug.

"You know something, Salvatore? You're crazy, " said Mrs. Bruno.

"No—just hungry. What's for supper?" He put his arm around his wife's waist and steered her toward the kitchen.

Paolo and his sister knelt next to the box and stared gravely at the new pet.

"What are you going to call him?" Gina asked.

"His name is Benvenuto."

"Hi, Benvenuto," said Gina, holding out her hand. She moved it forward very carefully, because she wasn't used to dragons yet. The little animal who, like most dragons, was extremely near-sighted, sniffed at the hand eagerly. He sniffed it all over. Then a small forked tongue crept out and began to lick the extended fingers.

"He's licking me! He's licking my hand!" Gina whispered.

"Dragons are a lot like dogs," Paolo explained.

Mrs. Bruno appeared at the kitchen doorway, a steaming bowl in her hands. "Supper's almost ready. You two can stop pestering that animal and go wash."

Benvenuto, sensing that he was at last an official member of the family, settled himself in the carton with his paws folded. His eyelids slowly drooped and he began to doze.

14

"What's that funny rumbling?" Gina asked.

"He's purring, stupid."

"*Purr*ing? But—"

"They're a lot like cats, too."

He and Gina jumped up, headed for the kitchen, and everybody settled down to supper. Mrs. Bruno bustled about the table, carrying hot pans and platters. She glanced into the living room, noticed the cardboard carton, and started muttering angrily once more. In the face of her discontent, the others fell silent.

Still grumbling, Mrs. Bruno sat down. Then she got up again, took an old cracked bowl from the pantry, and scooped some food into it.

"Here," she said, handing the bowl to Paolo, "maybe the lizard would like a little ravioli."

CHAPTER 2

PAOLO BUYS A LEASH

That night Benvenuto slept in the cardboard box, which Paolo put right next to his own cot. After the excitement of the day the whole family went to bed early and got a good night's rest. Except for Mrs. Bruno, who dreamed that a giant-sized Benvenuto was chasing her through Washington Square Park, snorting great blasts of smoke and flame.

First thing in the morning, before he even brushed his teeth, Paolo ran downstairs and got a fresh new carton from the grocery store. He turned it on its side, put it in a corner of his room, and spread an old blanket on the bottom. Then he took a black crayon and wrote on the carton in large letters:

For breakfast, Paolo, Gina and Benvenuto all had the same thing—puffed wheat with plenty of milk and sugar. Growing dragons need nourishment. They have very good appetites and, as Mrs. Bruno learned, will eat just about anything.

Halfway through his own breakfast, Paolo jumped up again.

"*Now* where are you going?" Mrs. Bruno asked.

"To buy a leash. So I can walk him," Paolo replied.

"Mama," Gina announced, "Paolo didn't brush his teeth."

Ignoring his sister, Paolo hurried out of the house. He walked along Bleecker Street to a little store that had a big sign over the door. The sign read:

OLGA'S
PET SHOPPE
GEWGAWS FOR PAWS & CLAWS
Madame Olga Foley, Prop.

Madame Olga was small and round. She had orange hair, wore yards and yards of enormous beads, and smoked Turkish cigarettes in a long ivory holder. Paolo and Madame Olga were friends. He had been to her shop many times last year during the parakeet episode. And before that, during the stray kitten incident. And before that, during the goldfish and turtle period.

When Paolo came in, Madame Olga gave him a friendly smile.

"You're my first customer today," she said, leaning her plump elbows on the glass counter. "What can I do for you, Paolo?"

"I need a leash," Paolo replied.

"Got a new puppy?"

Paolo shook his head. "No, not exactly."

"Kitten?"

"Nope," said Paolo.

"Don't tell me it's a monkey."

"No, not a monkey either."

Madame Olga nodded her head thoughtfully. She had managed her little store in Greenwich Village for a long, long time. When

19

it came to pets and people, nothing surprised her. Over the years, she had provided leashes for skunks and squirrels and minks and marmosets. She had sold cages for parrots and plovers and macaws and mynah birds. She had supplied glass tanks for box turtles and bull frogs and snakes and salamanders.

Madame Olga had sold harnesses for chimpanzees and ocelots. And once she had even stocked a supply of diapers for a baby gorilla who lived on Thompson Street with an artist named Crabtree.

But now she was curious.

"What *have* you got?" she asked. "A three-toed sloth?"

Paolo shook his head again. "It's more," he said, "along the lines of a dragon."

Madame Olga looked at Paolo for a long quiet moment. She puffed her cigarette and watched the smoke drift lazily toward the ceiling.

"A dragon," she said, half to herself.

"His name is Benvenuto," said Paolo.

"How big?"

Paolo held up his hands. "Like so. About the size of a small dog. He's practically a baby."

"This I have to see," Madame Olga mused. "This I really have to see. Will you bring him around some time? Soon?"

"Sure. Once I have a leash, I can take him anywhere."

Madame Olga came from behind the counter and joined Paolo. She poked a chubby hand among the leashes hanging on the rack.

"If I were you, St. George," she said, "I'd take one of these link chains. They're strong and they're fireproof."

Paolo picked out a shiny chain leash with a bright blue collar for $1.59 plus tax. He also bought two yellow plastic bowls, one for food and one for water. And with the 20 cents he had left, he bought a red rubber ball that had a little bell inside.

Madame Olga walked him to the door. "Good luck, St. George," she said. Paolo smiled at her and waved as he hurried down the street. She stood and watched him for a few moments, lost in thought.

"A dragon," she said to herself once more.

"It must be a lizard," she said to herself.

"Probably an iguana," she said to herself.

"But then again," she said to herself, "maybe it *is* a dragon. How do I know?"

Madame Olga shook her head as she walked back into her little store. "Boy," she thought, "this sure is an interesting neighborhood."

Paolo was so excited he ran most of the way home. As soon as he got in the house he put the new leash on Benvenuto. Gina, still in her pajamas, stood by and supervised.

"The collar just matches his blue eyes," she announced with approval.

Paolo tugged at the leash. "Come on, boy," he said. "It's time for your walk."

He started for the door with Benvenuto waddling at his heels. Then he stopped and turned toward the kitchen.

"Ma," he said, "who was St. George?"

Mrs. Bruno looked up from her pots and pans. She shrugged her shoulders. "*Io non so*," she said. "Ask papa tonight."

"*I* know," Gina chimed in. "He was a saint

in England, hundreds and hundreds of years ago. And he had this awful fight with this terrible dragon. And he killed it and became extremely famous."

"I figured something like that," Paolo said, heading out the door.

Benvenuto hesitated at the top of the stairs. His low-slung belly and his stubby little legs hadn't been designed for this sort of work. He started down nervously, almost lost his balance, and scrambled back in alarm. Then he looked up at Paolo and began to whimper.

Paolo bent over, scooped Benvenuto up in his arms, and trotted down the worn marble steps.

"You're a lucky guy," he said to Benvenuto, "that St. George never ran into *you*."

CHAPTER 3
BENVENUTO'S FIRST WALK

Keeping Benvenuto near the curb, Paolo walked a few blocks along Bleecker to Barrow Street. He turned up Barrow, strolled to the corner and then came down the other side.

Benvenuto didn't mind the noise and bustle of the big city. As long as Paolo was with him he felt calm and secure. And he caught on quickly to the main reason for their walk. So in *that* department the outing was a success.

For a while Paolo and his pet walked along contentedly. It was a clear morning and the August sun was warm and bright. Benvenuto sniffed and snuffed everywhere. The streets were rich with marvelous new smells, and he explored them all.

Among the new smells Benvenuto discovered that morning were garbage cans, lamp posts, fire hydrants, automobile tires, cigarette butts, an empty Coke bottle, the wrapper from an Almond Joy candy bar, a morsel of banana skin, a fragment of pizza pie, an abandoned sneaker (size 8½), and the soggy remains of a cold veal sandwich.

He also enjoyed the fine smells coming from the little shops along the street. There were fresh crisp smells from the vegetable market. Delicious warm smells from the bakery. Comfortable leathery smells from the shoe repair shop. Sharp pungent smells from the cheese store. And rich sweet smells from the corner florist.

Benvenuto, his tongue and nose busy, took it all in. But he wasn't the only one who made discoveries. Paolo also found out something.

He found out that you can walk a baby dragon on the streets of New York City, and most people won't even notice.

Of course, Paolo lived in an unusual neighborhood. In other parts of the city Benvenuto might have caused more excitement. But not in Greenwich Village. People there are very easy going. They are used to strange sights, and they have a "live and let live" kind of attitude. In that area just about anything goes. As long as you don't make too much fuss about it.

Some people—just a few—*did* notice Benvenuto. They would stop for a few moments and stare curiously at the little green animal. Then they would slowly walk on, a far-away look in their eyes.

Only one young man actually stopped and spoke to Paolo. He was wearing an Afro haircut and strumming an old beat-up guitar. When he saw Benvenuto he came over for a closer look.

"What you got there, baby?" he asked Paolo.

"It's sort of a dragon," Paolo replied.

"Cool," the young man said. "Very cool. Extremely and *su*premely cool." He patted Benvenuto gently on the head, then ambled on down the street, tuning his guitar strings.

That's how the morning went. Very calmly.
Very peacefully. Nobody caused any trouble
—not even the neighborhood dogs. In fact,
Benvenuto's first walk would have been perfect,
if it hadn't been for a little old man named
Guiseppe Tomaldo.

What happened was this. A big truck was
standing at the corner of Bleecker and Barrow,
waiting for a green light. Just as Paolo and Benvenuto reached the corner on their way home,
the truck driver raced his motor. And the truck
backfired loudly.

KA-POW!

The sudden noise scared the daylights out of Benvenuto. He had never heard a truck backfire before, and it threw him into a panic. Lunging from the curb, he rushed across the sidewalk. His only thought was to hide behind some garbage cans standing near the wall. At that very moment old Mr. Tomaldo came hurrying around the corner, carrying a large bag of groceries with a ripe cantaloupe perched on top.

Mr. Tomaldo, who didn't see too well to begin with, got his feet tangled in Benvenuto's leash. And down he went with a crash. The grocery

bag landed on the sidewalk too, and everything spilled out.

Paolo, upset by the incident, rushed over to help Mr. Tomaldo.

"I'm sorry," he apologized. "It was an accident. My pet just got scared, and—"

"Is okay," Mr. Tomaldo announced loudly. "Is okay."

The traffic light changed and the truck roared away, squashing Mr. Tomaldo's cantaloupe which had rolled into the gutter.

By this time, other people had gathered around. They got old Mr. Tomaldo back on his feet, dusted him off, and helped pick up the spilled groceries.

"I really *am* sorry, mister," Paolo said unhappily.

"Is okay," repeated Mr. Tomaldo. He was embarrassed by his spill. Which, he felt, was entirely due to his poor eyesight. Just then he caught sight of Benvenuto, cringing near the garbage cans and puffing nervous clouds of blue smoke.

Mr. Tomaldo bent down and patted Benvenuto's head.

"Nice doggie," he said. "Nice doggie. Not your fault."

He straightened his thin shoulders and marched off, clutching his grocery bag with dignity and continuing to announce loudly, "Is okay. Is okay."

Paolo picked Benvenuto up in his arms. The little animal was still trembling with fear, so Paolo decided to carry him the rest of the way home. Off they went, and that should have been the end of that.

But it wasn't, because something serious had happened. Something which Paolo failed to notice. When Mr. Tomaldo tripped over Benvenuto's leash, one of the little links in the chain had worked itself partway open. The link didn't break, but it had been badly damaged.

It was a very small link. So small that the damage never even caught Paolo's eye. But it was fated to cause a lot of trouble. Before long, the twisted link in Benvenuto's chain was to set off a twisted chain of much bigger events.

The strange events would involve not only Paolo and his family. They would involve Olga Foley, the pet shop lady. They would involve Patrolman Harry Fisher and Sergeant Orville Peck of the Sixth Police Precinct.

Also Dr. Philip O'Hara and Inspector Martin Weiss of the A.S.P.C.A. And Mr. Carlsen of the Central Park Zoo. And Dr. Waldo Collier, the Chief Veterinarian of the Board of Health.

And Judge Bayard C. Osgood of the State Supreme Court. And half the New York City Council. And finally the Mayor himself.

All these people, and more, would soon get involved. But nothing had happened so far, and no one knew about the problems that were coming. So Benvenuto finally calmed down. The morning ended at last. And nobody was really upset.

Nobody except Mr. Tomaldo, who got all the way home before he noticed that his nice ripe cantaloupe was missing.

CHAPTER 4

THE ROY SELBY INCIDENT

The next few days passed smoothly, and Benvenuto fitted quickly into the household routine.

He ate three good meals every day—mostly Alpo dog food, plus whatever leftovers he was given from the family table. He enjoyed everything he ate but loved Mrs. Bruno's ravioli best of all. Whenever she made it Benvenuto would sit at the kitchen door, watching her with moist eyes, the tip of his tail quivering with rapture.

Mrs. Bruno still grumbled about Benvenuto. But secretly she was growing quite fond of him.

And when nobody was watching she often slipped him little tid-bits from the pantry.

"I like a good eater," she would say to Mr. Bruno.

Benvenuto's legs grew stronger and soon he was able to manage the stairs by himself. Which was a relief to Paolo, because the little animal was getting heavier all the time.

Paolo discovered (through trial and error) that Benvenuto had to be walked twice a day. Once in the morning and once in the late afternoon. But Paolo was still on school vacation and had lots of time on his hands. So he took Benvenuto out more often than that.

Together, Paolo and his pet wandered happily through the neighborhood. From Carmine Street to Bank Street, and from Greenwich Avenue to Sheridan Square.

They paid a visit to Madame Olga at the pet shop. She marveled at Benvenuto and made a fuss over him.

"Fantastic," she kept murmuring.

And when they left she gave Benvenuto some biscuits from a box labelled PUPPY YUMMIES.

For the most part, people left them alone. Now and then a passerby would stop to talk to Paolo, or ask questions about Benvenuto. But everyone accepted the little dragon calmly. Even the police. The local cops were used to Greenwich Village and its strange ways. They just figured that Benvenuto was some kind of crazy looking lizard. As long as Paolo kept him on a leash and walked him near the curb, they were satisfied. And they let it go at that.

One pleasant afternoon, toward the end of August, Paolo led Benvenuto across Sixth Avenue and over to Washington Square Park. The park was one of Paolo's favorite places. Summer was ending, but the grass was still plentiful and the trees were thick with leaves.

They walked past a corner of the park where people sat and played chess. They walked past some hippies who were tossing a frisbee. They walked past some students from N.Y.U. who were sitting on the benches and studying.

In one play area there were three small dirt hills. Next to the hills were some high metal poles. They had bars sticking out so you could climb all the way to the top. Paolo stopped at the play area. He felt it was childish, but he wanted very much to climb one of the poles. Just once, to try it out. But he had Benvenuto to think of. He knew he couldn't let go of Benvenuto's leash. So he lingered for a moment, then they went on.

At the Good Humor cart, Paolo bought a black raspberry creamsicle. He sat on a bench to eat it. A young man and woman were also on the bench. They both had long hair and were wearing sandals, blue jeans, and tie-dye shirts. The young man was playing a wooden flute. The girl was singing in a soft sweet voice. When she saw Benvenuto she stopped singing and studied him.

"That," she said to Paolo, "is a beautiful animal. Does he have a pedigree?"

Paolo shrugged. He wasn't quite sure what a pedigree was.

"I found him this summer," he said. "In a cave."

The girl nodded gravely. "He's pure-bred, all right. You can always tell with dragons."

The young couple got up and sauntered off. Paolo finished his creamsicle and gave Benvenuto the stick to lick. As he looked up again a frown crossed his face.

Roy Selby was coming toward them. Roy was a kid in Paolo's class. He was bigger than the other kids. He had fists like hams and little eyes that were set close together. Roy was a bully and nobody liked him. Now he came walking along the deserted path, carrying a heavy stick which he kept banging on the park fence railing.

He came straight over to Paolo and Benvenuto.

"What's *that*?" he asked Paolo. "What kind of dopey animal is *that*?"

"Leave him alone," said Paolo.

Roy poked his stick into Benvenuto's round belly. He poked hard. Confused, Benvenuto backed away.

"Cut it out, Selby," Paolo said.

Roy kept poking away at Benvenuto. "Dopey animal," he chanted. "Dopey animal. Dopey animal. Dopey, dopey, dopey—"

Benvenuto whimpered unhappily and crept under the bench.

"Quit pestering him," Paolo said. He jumped up and tried to snatch the stick out of Roy's hand.

"Yaah," replied Roy, which was his idea of a smart answer. He slipped a big foot behind Paolo's legs, pushed hard, and Paolo fell over backward.

"You big crumb!" Paolo shouted, starting to scramble to his feet.

Suddenly Benvenuto went into action. The attack on Paolo had touched off something deep inside him. It had triggered some ancient hidden force, long buried in his dragon memory. Crouching low to the ground, Benvenuto crept toward Roy. He bared his sharp little teeth and a growling sound came from his throat. Then he raised his head.

Whoosh!

Two quick jets of flame shot from his nostrils. Roy stepped back, startled. The flames didn't quite reach him, but he could feel their heat.

"Wow," he said. "Wow."

Benvenuto kept moving forward. He growled loudly and the weird jets of flame shot from his nostrils again. With a grunt of terror, Roy dropped his stick and raced out of the park. He ran as fast as he could, and didn't stop until he got all the way to Houston Street.

Benvenuto tried to go after him and Paolo had to pull hard on the leash to hold him back. This pulling, unknown to Paolo, put another strain on the weak chain link—the link which Mr. Tomaldo had already damaged.

It took a few minutes for Benvenuto to calm down. Paolo was surprised at what had happened, but he was proud of Benvenuto. "Good boy," he said, patting him on the head. "You're a terrific watch dragon."

Paolo decided not to say anything to the family about Benvenuto's flame-throwing stunt. It was the sort of thing that they might not understand. Besides, Benvenuto was a gentle creature. Somehow, Paolo sensed that the flames would never be used except in serious emergencies.

As they left the park and started home, Paolo

felt pleased. Roy Selby had been taught a good lesson. He was sure they had seen the last of him. But as it turned out, Roy was to play an important part in coming events.

Old Mr. Tomaldo had been the first link in the approaching chain of troubles. Roy Selby was soon to be the second.

CHAPTER 5

DISAPPEARANCE OF BENVENUTO

T wo days later Paolo and Benvenuto found themselves back in Washington Square Park. It was late afternoon, and Paolo had gone on an errand for his mother. A friend of hers who lived a few blocks away was sick in bed. So she had sent him over with a large jar of homemade soup.

On his way home Paolo cut through the park. He headed right for the play area with the little hills and the climbing poles. In the gathering dusk the poles looked very challenging. Childish or not, Paolo was dying to try them.

"One quick climb," he said to himself, "just for a minute."

He twisted Benvenuto's leash around the metal park railing and tied several big knots in it.

"You be good," he said to Benvenuto.

Then he hurried over and started to climb one of the poles. It turned out to be very satisfying. In fact, Paolo had such a good time that he forgot to watch Benvenuto. Which was a shame. Because, while his back was turned, who should come strolling along but Roy Selby.

Roy and Benvenuto spotted each other at the very same moment. Roy stopped dead in his tracks. He stood there, shifting his feet uneasily. Benvenuto went into a crouch. Smoke curled from his nostrils. Then he lunged forward. Roy turned and ran. The little dragon lunged angrily again. The weak link gave way at last. The leash broke and suddenly Benvenuto was free. Moving rapidly on his stubby legs, he chased after Roy. Out of the park he went. Out into the gathering darkness.

When Paolo came down the pole a few minutes later and found Benvenuto gone, he was heartsick. He raced up and down the paths of the park, looking in every direction, and calling at the top of his lungs.

"Benvenuto!" he shouted. "Benvenuto! Here, boy!"

Paolo searched the park from one end to the other. Panting for breath, he scoured the nearby streets.

"Benvenuto! Benvenuto!"

Now it was quite dark and the lamp posts scattered unfriendly shadows along the sidewalks. There were endless doorways and alleys where Benvenuto could have wandered. Paolo hunted and hunted. But the little dragon was nowhere to be found. Benvenuto was gone. Swallowed up in the silent darkness of the big city.

When Paolo got home and broke the news, there was quite a fuss. Gina cried. Mrs. Bruno started muttering to herself in Italian. Mr. Bruno paced up and down, scratching his chin thoughtfully.

"It's *your* fault," Gina said to Paolo between sobs. "You should have made a tag for his collar. With his name and address on it."

Paolo felt so miserable he didn't even try to answer.

"Okay, okay," Mr. Bruno said. "Let's eat. Then we'll go out and look around some more."

The meal was over quickly because nobody felt hungry. Then Mr. Bruno, Paolo, and Gina hurried downstairs again to look for Benvenuto. They walked up and down the streets, calling his name and whistling. Gina even brought along a small bowl of ravioli, hoping that the odor would lure Benvenuto into the open.

The great Benvenuto hunt went on for hours. They searched and searched. They looked everyplace. But the little animal was nowhere to be seen. Worn out and weary, the hunters finally returned home.

Paolo couldn't believe that Benvenuto was really gone. Silently he pulled off his clothes. Then he climbed into bed and lay with his face buried in the pillow.

A few minutes later his father came in. Mr. Bruno sat on the edge of the cot and put his big hairy hand over Paolo's.

"Don't feel bad, *caro*," he said. "We'll find him. You'll see. We'll think of something. Don't you worry. Leave it to papa."

Paolo couldn't answer. But he held the big comfortable hand and squeezed it as tightly as he could.

He fell asleep still holding his father's hand.

CHAPTER 6

SPREADING THE WORD

Early next morning, before Mr. Bruno went to work, the family held a conference. Lots of ideas were tossed back and forth. Most of the ideas came from Gina. And many of them (like searching for Benvenuto by helicopter) were not very practical.

What it finally boiled down to was this. Mrs. Bruno would drop in on all the local storekeepers, most of whom she knew well. She would alert them to Benvenuto's disappearance, make careful inquiries, and try to pick up information. Paolo and Gina would visit

Madame Olga and ask if they could put a sign in her window. Mr. Bruno, who worked in a large bakery uptown, would stop at the offices of the *Village Voice* on his way home. The *Voice* was a neighborhood newspaper. He would arrange to place an ad about Benvenuto in the paper's Lost and Found column.

"I think we should give a reward," Gina said.

Mrs. Bruno seconded this. "A reward is a good idea."

"Okay," said Mr. Bruno. "We give a reward —maybe five dollars. But it comes out of Paolo's allowance."

Paolo nodded in agreement. That was fair. The whole thing was really his fault. And to get Benvenuto back again he would have given up his allowance for a year.

Madame Olga was very upset when she heard the news.

"The poor little thing," she sighed. "The poor little thing. Wandering around this crazy city."

She thought it was a fine idea to put a sign in the window of the pet shop. "But it has to be worded just right," she said. "When you

advertise for a lost dragon you have to use tact. Even in Greenwich Village."

With help from Paolo and Gina, Madame Olga made up the sign. She printed it on a piece of cardboard and taped it on the front window. It read:

LOST - ONE DRAGON
LAST SEEN IN AREA OF WASHINGTON SQUARE PARK

RESEMBLES A LARGE LIZARD
ANSWERS TO NAME "BENVENUTO"

HARMLESS, FRIENDLY

GENEROUS REWARD
CONTACT MADAME OLGA IN SHOP
(THIS IS NOT A JOKE)

"Now you kids cheer up," Madame Olga said as Paolo and his sister left the shop. "He may come home all by himself."

"You think so?" Paolo asked.

The pet shop lady shrugged. "It's possible. You told me yourself he's a lot like a cat. And you know how cats are. They have amazing instincts. A cat hardly ever forgets where it lives."

"I hope," sighed Paolo, "that Benvenuto doesn't forget 258 Bleecker Street."

That evening, over the kitchen table, the family compared notes. People in the neighborhood had all been alerted. The sign was up in the pet shop. The ad would appear in the next issue of the paper. They had done everything they could, and now they would have to wait.

"There's one more thing," Mr. Bruno said. "Tomorrow Paolo should go to the police station."

"The police?" asked Mrs. Bruno. *"Perche?"*

"They might know something," Mr. Bruno explained. "Maybe somebody reported Benvenuto. Or turned him in. He might be at the station right now."

Paolo looked at his father with interest.

"Benvenuto," continued Mr. Bruno, "isn't like a dog or a cat. People see a dog wandering around, or a cat—they pay no attention. The city is full of dogs and cats. Maybe they're strays. Maybe the owners don't want them any more. Who cares? But Benvenuto is unusual. If somebody sees him, he thinks, 'A very rare animal. Very valuable. Maybe it even belongs to the zoo.' So what does he do? He takes it to the police."

"Papa's right," Gina announced.

Paolo nodded. "Okay, I'll go tomorrow."

Mr. Bruno thumbed through the phone book. "Here it is," he said. "The Sixth Precinct. On West Tenth Street. Just a few blocks away."

That night Paolo had a frightening dream. He dreamed that he was at the police station. He was sitting in a hard wooden chair. Bright glaring lights were shining in his face. A lot of cops were standing in a ring around him.

"Confess!" they shouted at Paolo. "Confess!"

"Confess what?" Paolo asked. "I didn't *do* anything."

"Where's poor little Benvenuto?" they demanded.

"I told you," said Paolo. "He just ran away. Honest. It was an accident."

"What did you do with him?" they shouted angrily. "Confess! Confess!"

Paolo begged and pleaded but the police wouldn't listen. In his dream their angry faces grew bigger and bigger. And their angry voices grew louder and louder. And Paolo was awfully glad when he finally woke up.

CHAPTER 7

A VISIT TO THE POLICE

Sergeant Peck yawned loudly. He stretched his arms, looked at the clock and sighed. Only 9:15 in the morning and he was already bored with the day.

Orville Peck liked being a policeman. He liked it very much. But things had begun to change. He had been happy as a lowly patrolman walking a beat. He had enjoyed talking to the shopkeepers. And settling minor squabbles. And untangling traffic problems. And keeping the neighborhood sort of running smoothly.

On a neighborhood beat there was always

something happening. But now that he was a three-striper, he spent most of his time sitting behind a big precinct desk. Away from his friends. Away from all the action. Sure, his job was necessary and important. But all he seemed to do was answer phones and wrestle with paperwork. And every day was just like the one before.

Halfway through another yawn he noticed two children coming through the big double doors. One was a boy about twelve years old. The other was a little girl. They looked alike, and Peck decided that they were brother and sister.

The children came over to the big desk hesitantly.

"What can I do for you, folks?" Sergeant Peck asked.

"It's about my pet," Paolo said.

"He got lost the day before yesterday," Gina explained. "In Washington Square Park."

Officer Peck slumped in his chair. Kids and their lost dogs. That's what his life work had come to.

"Sorry, folks," he said. "Nobody's brought in a dog for three or four days."

"This isn't exactly a dog," Paolo replied.

The Sergeant sat up a bit straighter.

"What did you lose?" he asked.

"Well, it's sort of—you might say it looks like a lizard. A big lizard," said Paolo.

"But it's not a lizard," added Gina. "It's really a dragon."

Sergeant Peck slumped again.

"Oh. Well, we don't collect lost *toys* here," he said. "For toys you'll have to check with—"

Paolo shook his head. "Benvenuto isn't a toy. He's real."

"He's a real dragon, all right," said Gina. "He has green scales and a long tail and blue smoke comes out of his nose. If you don't believe us, ask Madame Olga. She owns the pet shop."

Peck stared at them. Then he turned his head.

"Hey, Harry," he called, "come here a minute."

A young policeman left a group standing at the bulletin board and walked over. He was tall and skinny and had sandy hair and a big walrus mustache.

"What's up, Orv?" he asked.

The Sergeant turned to Paolo and Gina. "Tell Patrolman Fisher what you just told me."

"I lost my pet," said Paolo. "He looks like a big lizard."

"Only he's really a dragon," said Gina.

"If you don't believe them," Peck added, "just ask Madame Olga who runs the pet shop."

"Olga Foley? On Bleecker Street?"

Paolo nodded. "She's our friend. She let us put up a sign in her window."

"We're giving a reward," said Gina. "It's coming out of Paolo's allowance."

Patrolman Fisher looked at Sergeant Peck. "What's the gag, Sarge?"

"It isn't a gag, sir," Paolo said hastily. "It's the truth. Honest." He described Benvenuto in careful detail to the two policemen. Then he explained the events that led to the animal's disappearance. He told about tying Benvenuto to the railing, and climbing the pole, and then coming back to find the broken leash.

Patrolman Fisher suddenly snapped his fingers. "I know you," he said. "Of course. You're the kid with the lizard."

Peck grinned and reached for the phone. "I'll check with the A.S.P.C.A. Maybe your friend wandered into another precinct."

"We don't keep animals here in the station house," Harry Fisher explained to the kids. "Whenever we get a stray dog or cat or anything, we call the A.S.P.C.A. And they come pick it up."

The Sergeant spoke into the phone. "Charlie? This is Peck at the Sixth Precinct. Listen. You got anything up there that looks like a big lizard? Or a small dragon? . . . Of *course* I'm serious . . . Yeh. About two feet long, including the tail . . . I know, I know . . . Well, we have two kids here and that's what they told us. They lost him a couple of days ago . . . Yeh, it sure is . . . If anything turns up let me know, will you?"

Sergeant Peck hung up and turned to Paolo and Gina. "I'm sorry. The A.S.P.C.A. hasn't got him."

Gina's eyes suddenly filled with tears. "Paolo, maybe Benvenuto got run over," she said. "Maybe he's dead."

"Cut it out," Paolo muttered. But he was worried himself. Maybe his little pet was hungry. Maybe he was frightened. He knew that Benvenuto liked warm cozy places. And now he might be huddled in some dark and lonely corner, shivering with the cold. Paolo fought hard to keep back his own sudden tears.

"Listen," the Sergeant said, "why don't we fill out a Lost Property Report? Okay? We don't usually do this for pets. But this is a special case."

Peck took a long complicated form from his desk, with lots of carbon pages attached. Under TYPE OF LOST ARTICLE he wrote *dragon*. Under NAME OR TRADEMARK he wrote *Benvenuto*. Under QUANTITY he wrote *one*. Under VALUE he wrote *not known*. Then he wrote a description of Benvenuto, just as Paolo had given him.

"We'll keep this on file," he said when he finished. "You can never tell. He might turn up anytime. If we hear anything, we'll get right in touch with you."

The policemen watched as the two children walked out, Gina with her hand in Paolo's. Patrolman Fisher stroked his big moustache nervously.

"Even if they find him," he said, "they probably won't be allowed to keep him."

The Sergeant shrugged. "That's the Health Department's problem. They make the rules. But put a notice on the bulletin board, Harry. And tell Shiffman to make an announcement at the squad turn-out. I don't like the idea of that thing wandering around loose in the precinct."

Orville Peck chuckled to himself. "Peck, the dragon hunter," he thought. Well, in a way it had been the most interesting morning he'd had in a long long time.

Meanwhile Charlie Dobbs, the desk man at the A.S.P.C.A., was sitting and brooding. He was brooding about Sergeant Peck's phone call. Finally he decided to go upstairs and talk to Dr. O'Hara.

Philip O'Hara was an animal doctor. His job was to take care of the many dogs and cats at the A.S.P.C.A. He gave them shots, patched up injuries, set broken bones, and checked them for various diseases. Sometimes an unusual animal—such as a monkey or an ocelot—would turn up. After a while, if nobody came to claim it, Dr. O'Hara would have the animal sent to a city zoo.

Dr. O'Hara was a worrier. He worried about dogs with rabies and cats with distemper. He worried about squirrels biting people and birds carrying parrot fever. When he heard what Charlie Dobbs had to say, he started worrying again.

Alone in his office he paced up and down, polishing his eyeglasses. He always polished his eyeglasses when he worried. And now he polished them briskly. Then he put in a call to his friend Carlsen, who ran the reptile house at the Central Park Zoo.

"Jim," he said, "this is O'Hara. Are you missing any lizards over there?"

"Missing any *what*?" came the response.

"Lizards. We just got a call from the Sixth Precinct. Some kids came in to report a lost lizard. And not one of those dinky little things. They told the desk officer it was two feet long and covered with green scales. There was some nonsense about it being a dragon. But what I want to know, are those things dangerous? Do they carry rabies?"

"Well, no," Carlsen replied. "They're not likely to be carriers. But one or two species are poisonous. And some of them can bite."

"What about other diseases? Can you pick up a disease from a lizard?"

"Not if you don't kiss it," said Carlsen.

"Very funny," said Dr. O'Hara. "What do you think it is, anyway? What does it sound like to you?"

"Hard to say, Doc. It might possibly be a land iguana. Or maybe even a Tegu lizard. I hope it's not a Tegu. They're pretty vicious. And a Gila monster's even worse. A bite from one of those lizards can put you right in the hospital."

"I can't figure how they got it into the country, past Customs. Could one of yours have gotten loose somehow? Or been stolen?"

"No, not a chance," Carlsen said. "I'll check it right now. But I'm quite sure it isn't one of our babies."

By the time Dr. O'Hara hung up he was more worried than ever. After a moment he picked up the phone again.

"Sergeant Peck? This is Dr. O'Hara at the A.S.P.C.A. Listen, about those kids with the lizard. You think they were serious? I mean, it wasn't a prank or anything? . . . Uh, huh . . . Well, you'd better give me their name and address . . . Yes, thanks . . . I'm going to call the Chief Veterinarian at Worth Street. And we'll have to alert the other police precincts in Manhattan. Frankly, I don't like the sound of this. I don't like it at all."

On their way home from the station, Paolo did his best to cheer Gina up.

"Don't cry," he said. "We'll find him. You'll see. Maybe he'll come home all by himself, like Madame Olga said. And now we've got the police working on it."

Paolo had no way of knowing, but a lot of other people were also working on it. At that very moment, official phones were ringing all over the city of New York. Anxious questions and strange rumors were flying back and forth. And all of them were about the very same thing—a little lost animal named Benvenuto.

CHAPTER 8

RETURN OF THE WANDERER

Mr. Bruno came home from work waving a copy of the *Village Voice*. "Look, everybody. Benvenuto's name is in the paper!"

The family gathered around to look at the ad on the Lost and Found page. It read:

LOST—Vic. Washington Sq. Park
Animal resembling
FAIRY-TALE DRAGON
Has green scales and blows blue smoke.
Answers to name BENVENUTO.
Generous REWARD! Call 555–4451

"What do we do now, papa?" Gina asked.

"Now," Mr. Bruno said, "we wait. Maybe somebody will call up with good news."

The phone began ringing during supper. It rang quite a lot. Most of the callers announced that they were St. George, and offered their services. One lady phoned to say that she had eighteen stray cats. She thought they might like a nice kitten to take Benvenuto's place. Another caller tried to sell them a six foot boa constrictor. And one young man explained seriously that he hadn't seen their dragon, but wanted help in finding his pet unicorn.

By eight o'clock everyone was depressed. The ad had been a flop. Each time the phone rang, their hopes rose. And each time they had been badly disappointed.

To cheer them all up, Mr. Bruno decided to go out and buy ice cream. He patted Paolo's shoulder. "Come along," he said, "and keep me company."

On their way back with the ice cream, Paolo and his father had to pass a narrow alley alongside their building. As they walked by, Paolo heard a faint but familiar sound. He stopped. He listened as hard as he could.

There it was again—the sound of whimpering. Paolo held his breath. He peered into the dim alley. A large wooden packing crate was lying on its side. And from it came a thin wisp of blue smoke!

"Benvenuto!" Paolo shrieked. He dashed into the alley and dove headfirst into the crate. Sure enough, there was his pet—cowering in a corner and shivering with the cold.

Paolo scooped Benvenuto up in his arms and raced back to his father. "I found him!" he shouted. "I found him! Benvenuto came home!"

When they burst in the door of the apartment, pandemonium broke loose. Gina squealed and danced. Mr. Bruno marched around laughing. Mrs. Bruno hugged Paolo and muttered rapidly to herself in Italian. She hurried into the kitchen and put together a big platter of leftovers. Then everyone sat down and watched Benvenuto gobble it up.

They could tell that their wanderer was

glad to be home. But he looked thin. His eyes were bloodshot. And his usually neat coat of scales was dirty and scratched.

"He looks like he had a rough time," said Mr. Bruno.

"I bet he hasn't had a good meal for days," Paolo added.

"He shouldn't eat so fast," said Gina. "He'll vomit."

Just then the phone rang again.

"Another nut," grunted Mr. Bruno, picking up the receiver. But this time he was mistaken.

"Mr. Bruno?" a voice said. "This is Sergeant Peck at the Sixth Precinct. Sorry to bother you so late, but it's about that animal you lost—"

Paolo's father laughed. "Not lost any more," he said. "Thank you, Sergeant, but everything's okay now. We just found him. Just a little while ago."

"Oh. Well, that's fine. Fine. But listen, Mr. Bruno—I've been getting a lot of flak here. The Health Department's on my neck."

"The Health Department?"

"Yeh. They're kind of worried. We have this Health Code, you know. You're not allowed to keep wild animals in the city."

"Benvenuto isn't a wild animal. He's just a pet."

Sergeant Peck sounded uncomfortable. "Well, sure. It's probably okay. But we have to be careful. Someone from the A.S.P.C.A. has to come down there and look it over. If the animal isn't permissible, you have to get rid of it."

"Get rid of Benvenuto? But—"

"Sorry, Mr. Bruno. It's out of my hands now. The A.S.P.C.A. will send their people to check it out. That's the way it's done. You'll probably hear from them tomorrow."

When Mr. Bruno told the family what Sergeant Peck had said, their joy melted away. A pall of gloom settled over everyone. Suddenly worried, they looked at Benvenuto who was now dozing contentedly in a warm corner of the room.

"They *can't* take him away," Paolo said. "Not when we just *found* him."

"Don't worry, *caro*," Mr. Bruno replied. "Nobody's taking anybody away. Everything will be okay. You'll see."

He tried hard to smile, but the gloom became deeper. A sense of creeping doom settled over them—a dark feeling that there was trouble ahead.

Then Gina added the final touch. She came to the kitchen door holding up a soggy, dripping paper bag.

"Papa," she said, "we forgot all about the ice cream."

CHAPTER 9

AN OFFICIAL VISIT

The doorbell rang late the next afternoon. When Mr. Bruno answered it, he saw two strange men standing there. One was tall and thin, and was busily polishing his glasses. The other was short and had a round pink face. He wore a blue uniform.

"I'm Dr. O'Hara," the tall man said, "the veterinarian from the A.S.P.C.A. And this is Inspector Weiss, one of our Field Agents."

Mr. Bruno gave a courtly bow and invited them in. "Go get Benvenuto," he said to his son.

Paolo went to his room and came out with
Benvenuto. But first he put on the new leash
which had been a home-coming gift from
Madame Olga.

The two men stared at the little dragon. They
walked around him slowly. They looked him
over carefully. Benvenuto yawned and sat
down in the middle of the floor. Now that he
was home again he felt safe and happy, and
he didn't mind being studied by these two
strange men.

Dr. O'Hara bent down and held out his hand.
Benvenuto licked it calmly with his forked
tongue. Inspector Weiss ran expert fingers over
Benvenuto's scaly skin. He examined his paws.
He looked at his long pointy tail.

"Ha," said Dr. O'Hara.

"Hm," said Inspector Weiss.

"Well, it's not an iguana," said Dr. O'Hara.

"*No* way," said Inspector Weiss. "Not a Gila,
either. Or a Tegu. Tell you the truth—I've
never seen a lizard quite like this one before."

"Benvenuto isn't a lizard," said Gina. "He's
a dragon."

"Is he tame?" the doctor asked Paolo. "I mean, he doesn't bite? Or snap at people?"

"No, sir," replied Paolo. "He's very gentle. Very nice and friendly." He had a sudden memory of Roy Selby backing nervously away from two bright jets of flame—but Paolo decided not to mention *that*.

"What does he like to eat?" asked Dr. O'Hara.

"Lots of greens, I suppose? Parsley? Spinach? Lettuce?" asked Inspector Weiss.

"Well, he eats everything," Paolo said, "but mostly Alpo dog food."

"And mama's ravioli," Gina added.

The two men stared at her.

"My wife makes the best ravioli in the neighborhood," Mr. Bruno said proudly.

"Ha," said Dr. O'Hara.

"Hm," said Inspector Weiss.

All the talk of food had its effect on Benvenuto. He burped loudly, and two enormous blue smoke rings popped from his nostrils.

"HO!" said Dr. O'Hara.

"HEY!" said Inspector Weiss.

Dr. O'Hara polished his eyeglasses so hard

that he dropped them on the rug. Out came Benvenuto's tongue, and he licked them curiously.

"Does he do that often? The blue smoke thing?" asked Inspector Weiss, while the doctor retrieved his glasses.

"Now and then," said Paolo. "Mostly when he's tired."

"Or scared," said Gina.

"Or hungry," added Mrs. Bruno.

"Ha," said Dr. O'Hara.

"Hm," said Inspector Weiss.

He took a booklet out of his pocket. "You understand, Mr. Bruno, we're not out to cause you trouble. Or unnecessary bother. We just have to be careful. There are a lot of people in this city, and they have to be protected. The animals have to be protected, too."

Inspector Weiss flipped the pages of the little book. "This covers all the animal laws for New York," he continued. "There are lots of wild animals that just aren't allowed in the city. Lions, tigers, jaguars, wildcats, raccoons, bears, poisonous snakes. And iguanas, too."

"The problem," said Dr. O'Hara, "is that a wild animal can never be fully tamed. They're never really safe. So according to law, when we find a family with a wild animal, we tell them they have to give it up."

"Give it up how?" asked Mr. Bruno.

"Well, it has to be sent to one of the zoos. Or sold to a professional pet dealer. Then he places it with a circus. Or maybe a carnival."

"Or he might sell it to an animal laboratory," added Inspector Weiss.

"A laboratory? Where they cut them *up*?!" Gina shrieked.

"*Mamma mia!*" gasped Mrs. Bruno.

"Never!" growled Mr. Bruno. "Never!"

Dr. O'Hara shot an irritated glance at Inspector Weiss.

"No, of course not," he said quickly. "There's no need for anything drastic. I'm sure the Bronx Zoo would take him. Or the Central Park Zoo. Or the one on Staten Island. Staten Island is always looking for new specimens."

"You can't put Benvenuto in a cage," Paolo said unhappily. "He would *die* there!"

"Now, don't get upset," Dr. O'Hara replied. "We're not saying for sure that you can't keep him."

"This is an unusual case," sighed Inspector Weiss.

"Very unusual," added Dr. O'Hara. "Of course, we'll have to talk this over with the Health Department people. They're the ones who make the final decision."

Inspector Weiss handed the little booklet to Mr. Bruno. "You might like to have this," he said.

The two men took one last look at Benvenuto, said goodnight and left the apartment. They walked downstairs lost in thought.

"Ha," said Dr. O'Hara.

"Hm," said Inspector Weiss.

Madame Olga stopped in at the Bruno's later that evening. When she heard about the visit she frowned.

"I don't like it," she said. "I'm going to get in touch with my friend, Luther Lewis. He's a young lawyer. Smart as a whip. And he owes me a few favors. We might need him."

"You really think so?" asked Mr. Bruno.

"And how," said Madame Olga. "Take it from me—when the city gets into the act, you're in for headaches. I'm pretty sure we haven't heard the last of this."

A silence fell over the group. A heavy silence, broken only by the gentle sound of Benvenuto purring on the rug.

CHAPTER 10
"LET THE DEFENDANT SHOW CAUSE—"

One week later the blow fell.

School had started at last, and Paolo and Gina were in their rooms doing homework. Benvenuto was resting in his box. Mr. Bruno was dozing on the couch. Mrs. Bruno was puttering around the kitchen.

When the doorbell rang, Gina jumped up to answer it. She recognized Patrolman Harry Fisher from the police station. Another man, a stranger, was with him.

"Hi," said Officer Fisher. "Is your father home?"

Mr. Bruno, sleepy-eyed, poked his head around the door.

The man with Officer Fisher was holding an official looking paper with a red seal on it.

"Salvatore M. Bruno?" he asked.

"Speaking," said Mr. Bruno.

"I am a City Marshal, sir," the man continued. "It is my duty to serve you with this court order." Then he handed the paper to Mr. Bruno.

Officer Fisher looked embarrassed. "I'm sorry, folks," he said, "but all we do is carry out orders."

When the two men left, the family gathered around Mr. Bruno. He unfolded the legal paper and looked it over, mumbling to himself. Now and then he read part of it out loud.

"City of New York, Plaintiff," he read, "against Salvatore M. Bruno, Defendant . . . upon the annexed petition of Dr. Philip O'Hara and Field Inspector Martin D. Weiss, sworn to this day . . ."

"I don't understand all those big words," said Gina.

". . . let the Defendant show cause," Mr. Bruno went on, "before Special Term, Part I, at 9:30 in the forenoon on September 18th . . . why he, Salvatore M. Bruno, should not deliver up: *one lizard (species unknown)* to the A.S.P.C.A. for disposal . . . Sufficient cause appearing therefore, service of this order is directed by the Honorable Bayard C. Osgood, Justice."

"What does it mean, papa?" asked Paolo.

"I think it means trouble for Benvenuto," sighed Mrs. Bruno.

"Trouble for *them*, too," said Mr. Bruno, setting his jaw grimly. *"Nobody's* going to take Benvenuto away from us."

That night a council of war took place in the Bruno's living room. Madame Olga came over in answer to a hasty phone call. And she brought her friend, Luther Lewis, with her.

Luther Lewis was a bright young black lawyer. Most of his legal work had to do with civil rights cases and community problems.

Everyone (including Benvenuto) sat in a circle while Luther read the court order. When he finished, he nodded his head. "This is standard stuff," he explained. "It's called a 'show cause' order. You see, the A.S.P.C.A. and the Health Department want Benvenuto put away. But first the court gives you a chance to be heard. If this Judge Osgood decides in our favor, you keep Benvenuto. If he decides against us, Benvenuto has to go."

"What if we don't do what the judge says?" asked Mr. Bruno.

Luther frowned. "That's a real hassle. If you disobey the ruling, you're in contempt of court. It can mean a jail sentence. And a stiff fine."

"They'd never put Benvenuto in jail," scoffed Gina.

Paolo hooted at her. "Not Benvenuto, dummy. *Papa*."

"So what do we do now?" asked Madame Olga.

Luther stood up and started pacing. "Let's see. We're due in court on the 18th. That gives us a week to work out our strategy."

Suddenly he stopped and snapped his fingers. "Got it! Sure! We'll challenge the right of the courts to judge Benvenuto!"

"*Non capisco*," said Mrs. Bruno. "I don't understand."

"It's simple," said Luther. He picked up the little booklet which Inspector Weiss had given to Mr. Bruno.

"Here," he said. "Take a look at Section 161.01 of the New York City Health Code. It lists all the wild animals which are *not* permitted in the city. *But it doesn't say anything about dragons!*"

"Luther's right!" squealed Gina. "Luther's right!"

"The court order," Luther went on, "refers to 'one lizard (species unknown)'. Well, Benvenuto isn't a lizard at all. He's a dragon. And dragons just aren't covered by the City code."

"I think you've got something there," said Madame Olga, excited.

Luther rubbed his hands. "What we'll do is collect a pile of letters and affadavits. We'll get statements from lots of people about how kind and gentle Benvenuto is. We'll present them all to the judge. And then we'll clinch it by pointing out that Benvenuto doesn't even come under the law. So they have no right to bother us. I don't know if it'll work. But it's worth a try."

"I'll help collect the letters," Madame Olga said.

"Me, too!" cried Gina.

Paolo dropped to his knees. He stroked Benvenuto gently. "Don't you worry," he said. "Just leave everything to Mr. Lewis."

Mr. Bruno stood up, grabbed Luther's hand, and shook it firmly. "You're a good man," he said. *"Grazie.* Thank you for helping us."

Luther grinned. "Don't mention it. My job is defending minority groups. And I guess dragons are the tiniest minority of all."

CHAPTER 11

FAME FOR BENVENUTO

New York is the kind of place where rumors and gossip travel fast. Someone tells a bit of news to a friend. The friend tells his wife. His wife tells the corner grocer. The corner grocer tells a customer. The customer tells her husband. Her husband tells a taxi driver. And soon everyone in town knows what's going on.

So it wasn't long before the newspapers found out about Benvenuto. And in no time at all, the Feature Editor of the *Daily News* phoned Mr. Bruno. He said that he wanted to do a story about Benvenuto, and asked if he could send down a reporter and a photographer.

Mr. Bruno thought it over. He decided that a reporter would be okay. But he didn't want a photographer in the house. He was afraid that the popping flashbulbs would frighten Benvenuto. And they might harm his weak eyes.

The reporter from the newspaper turned out to be an attractive young lady with long blonde hair and huge tinted eyeglasses. She chewed the end of her pencil, scribbled lots of notes on her pad, and said "Oh, wow!" every time she looked at Benvenuto.

She stayed for an hour, then left. But not before she had accepted an invitation from Mrs. Bruno to come back soon for dinner.

The *Daily News* carried the story on Page 3 of the morning edition. It read:

ATTENTION, ST. GEORGE! DRAGON INVADES GREENWICH VILLAGE!

Paolo Bruno, age 12, believes in dragons. So much so that he brought one home from camp with him last month.

The "dragon," a strange

looking lizard-like creature, lives with the Bruno family at 258 Bleecker Street, in the heart of Greenwich Village. It measures some two feet in length, from its nose to the tip of its long scaly tail.

The dragon's name is "Benvenuto" and it lives chiefly on dog food and ravioli. According to the Brunos, it also puffs blue smoke, but this reporter did not have the good luck to see a demonstration.

City officials are attempting to have the animal removed, on the grounds that it is a dangerous species and not on the city's "permissible pet" list. Dr. Waldo Collier, Chief Veterinarian of the N. Y. Department of Health, is playing it close to the bureaucratic chest. "This office has no comment," he stated. "The matter is now in the hands of the courts."

The Brunos plan to fight for the right to keep their beloved pet. Their lawyer, Luther Lewis, is busy preparing a strong defense.

Are dragons really unwelcome in Fun City? Say it ain't so, Dr. Collier!

That night, Benvenuto made television. Howard B. Stokely, the popular newscaster, talked about the case on his local TV show, "New York Reporting." He described Benvenuto, gave the general facts, and explained that the city was planning to take action.

And on the following morning there was an editorial in the *New York Times*. It read:

IN SEARCH OF CHILDHOOD

It has come to our attention that the City of New York now has a real live dragon in residence. The dragon was brought home from summer camp by a Greenwich Village youngster named Paolo Bruno.

However, the Health Department has taken a dim view of this unusual pet, and wants it tucked away safely behind bars.

The matter, we understand, will soon be decided by the courts. Which is a wise approach. After all, the city must protect its citizens against dangerous animals. But, in this case, can we not temper justice with mercy? And with imagination?

Over the years, New York has survived crime waves, strikes, riots, blizzards, water shortages, traffic crises and power failures. Can we not also survive the presence of one small dragon?

In Western literature, dragons are presented as fierce and frightening creatures. But in the Far East, they are looked upon as kind protectors, and symbols of good luck. We are sure that Paolo Bruno's little pet is of the Oriental breed.

Dragons, elves, fairy godmothers, witches, knights in shining armor—all these are the stuff of childhood. The roots of myth and fantasy. They call to mind stories of romance and courage, of honor and nobility.

We refuse to believe that these happy qualities are dead and gone. We know that somewhere in this troubled world they are still alive. If only in the pages of fairy tales. If only in the hearts of children.

Yes, Paolo—there *are* dragons. Never, never doubt it.

All these reports stirred up quite a lot of interest in Benvenuto. To the great surprise of the Brunos, letters and postcards began pouring in. One or two were critical. The writers felt that Benvenuto was a menace and should be put away. Along with every dog, cat, rabbit, bird, hamster, and gerbil in the city of New York.

But most of the letters were on the Bruno's side. The writers pledged their full support, and many even sent money.

Letters flooded in containing dimes, quarters and dollar bills. The 6th grade students of P.S. 45 in Brooklyn collected $18.73 in an old cigar box, and sent it to help pay Benvenuto's court fees. One couple in Queens sent a check for $40 with a note that said simply, "Fight the good fight." The children of Paolo's and Gina's school also took up a collection for the "Benvenuto Defense Fund."

There were many gifts, too. People sent in fruit cakes, and small knitted sweaters, and fancy leashes, and cans of dog food, and little toys for Benvenuto. And one lady in Connecticut sent a large box of homemade carrot cookies, all shaped like little dragons.

The Benvenuto case even reached all the way to City Hall. A member of the City Council (who happened to live in Greenwich Village) introduced a bill to exempt Benvenuto from the City Health Code. But the bill never came to a vote. After a lively debate, it was sent to the Environmental Controls Board for further study.

Later that day, reporters asked the Mayor himself for comments on the case.

The Mayor smiled. "I'm sorry," he said, "but I can't say anything while the matter is before the courts. We must let justice take its course. But I'm not worried, either way. In my job you get to do battle with dragons every day."

The Bruno family could hardly believe what was happening. Almost overnight, Benvenuto had become famous. Now, when Paolo took his pet for a walk, a crowd quickly gathered. People patted Paolo on the back and wished him good luck. And some even asked him for his autograph.

Mr. Bruno grumbled a little about all the fuss. But Madame Olga was delighted.

"The publicity will help our case," she said. "It's a real ground swell. We've got the people behind us!"

Luther Lewis was a lot more realistic. "Listen," he said at the next meeting of the war council, "all this publicity is fine. We're getting plenty of support from the public. But we still have to face Judge Osgood. *He's* the one who'll have the last word. And I hear he's a tough character. Takes everything *very* seriously. So let's remember the old saying: 'Don't count your chickens before they're hatched.' "

"Or your dragons, either," sighed Paolo.

CHAPTER 12

JUDGE OSGOOD DECIDES

On the day of the court hearing everyone got up early. The past week had been an exciting one. But now they all felt tense and nervous. Nobody ate any breakfast. Except Benvenuto, who had his usual bowl of dog food plus a little left-over macaroni.

They dressed quietly. Paolo put on his good suit. Mr. Bruno wore his new purple tie. And Gina tied a big blue ribbon around Benvenuto's neck.

At the last minute, Luther Lewis had decided to take Benvenuto with them.

"The court order doesn't say we should bring him," he explained, "but it might help."

Luther came by at 8:30. Then they all piled into Madame Olga's station wagon and drove silently to the gray stone courthouse on Foley Square.

Room 403, where the case was to be heard, was packed with people. There were reporters and photographers, and a great many well-wishers. Paolo recognized lots of neighborhood friends in the crowd.

The Brunos were given seats in the first row, just behind the wooden railing. The room buzzed with excited chatter. But a sudden hush fell and everyone stood up as the judge entered.

Judge Bayard C. Osgood looked very stern in his black robes. He was a heavy-set man with gray hair and cold eyes. Paolo swallowed hard. Judge Osgood didn't look like a friendly man. Certainly not the sort who would be kind to little dragons.

Frowning, the judge looked around the court-room. Then he nodded to the court clerk. The clerk announced in a loud voice, "The People

of the City of New York versus Salvatore M. Bruno!"

Luther and the lawyer for the City of New York stood up and they both approached the bench.

The city lawyer spoke first. His job was to give the Health Department's point of view. He called the judge's attention to the City Health Code. Here it was all carefully spelled out. Certain wild animals simply were not permitted in the city. Experience had shown that these health laws were sound and valuable. Many wild animals were disease carriers. And some were quite dangerous.

The lawyer produced statements from various doctors and hospitals. They told of cases in which city people had been clawed or bitten by animals such as wildcats, raccoons, chimpanzees, ocelots, and lion cubs.

Besides this, the lawyer went on, the animals themselves suffered. Keeping them in the city was cruel and unfair. A big city was no place for wild creatures to live.

For all these reasons, he said, the authorities

felt that Benvenuto should be taken away from the Bruno family. And without delay.

When the city lawyer finished, Luther was given a chance to answer. He handed the judge a batch of statements from Madame Olga and many other friends. They all described Benvenuto's gentle manner and his kindly disposition. He was, Luther explained, an extremely tame and well-behaved animal.

Luther told how Paolo had found Benvenuto starving in the woods. And how he had nursed him back to health. He described the great love and care which the Brunos had given their little pet. Then he asked Paolo to step forward with Benvenuto.

Holding tightly to the leash, Paolo led Benvenuto out of the row of seats and up to the judge's bench. The spectators all craned their necks, and Paolo felt hundreds of eyes on him. Even the judge stood up and leaned over to get a better look.

Benvenuto, not the least bit bothered, squinted up at the judge. His tail wagged in a friendly greeting.

"Hrmmph," said Judge Osgood.

When Paolo and Benvenuto sat down again, Luther made his final point. He challenged the right of the Health Department to bring the Brunos to court. Benvenuto, Luther pointed out, wasn't even on the wild animal list. He was not a "lizard (species unknown)" but actually a dragon. Many respectable people firmly believed this. Even Dr. O'Hara and Inspector Weiss agreed that they had never seen a creature like Benvenuto. And they were experts.

Luther told of the many letters that had poured in. These people all accepted the fact that Benvenuto was indeed a dragon. They hoped that the Brunos could keep him, and go on taking care of him.

Luther Lewis spoke eloquently and movingly.

"Your Honor," he said, "Paolo Bruno and his family have earned the right to keep this remarkable pet. Counsel submits that the animal is not a menace. We also believe that there is a great deal at stake here. This is not a small matter. There are many who claim that New

York has lost something precious. That it has become a hard, cold, uncaring place. Let us hope that today's decision will prove them wrong. Let us hope it will show them that our city, with all its problems, still has a feeling heart."

When Luther sat down, a hush fell over the big room. All eyes were on Judge Osgood. Paolo held his breath. Gina and Mrs. Bruno clutched each other's hands. Mr. Bruno scratched his chin very slowly.

The judge leaned back in his big leather chair. He stared at the ceiling for a long long moment. Then he leaned forward and cleared his throat. His face was still stony.

"This is an unusual situation," he said. "Most unusual. The court understands the concern of the Health Department. And we fully approve. The city must protect its citizens. We certainly cannot allow dangerous animals to roam our streets at will . . ."

Paolo's heart sank. The judge sounded angry. He was going to make them put Benvenuto away!

". . . on the other hand," for the first time a slight smile crossed Judge Osgood's face, "counsel for the defense has pointed out quite rightly that dragons are *not* mentioned in the City Health Code."

The judge's eyes began to twinkle.

"To my knowledge, the City of New York has never clearly spelled out its policy concerning dragons. I find this a shocking oversight. But nevertheless a fact. And one which the court cannot ignore."

Judge Osgood leaned forward and grew more serious.

"The court is also impressed with the loving care and devotion given this animal by the Bruno family. It is obvious that they are aware of their responsibilities: both to the animal and to the community. As long as this family continues to take good and proper care of their pet, I see no reason to take further action. The case is dismissed. The Brunos and their—ah—dragon are free to go."

When Judge Osgood finished, the courtroom exploded. The crowd cheered and

106

applauded. Mr. Bruno hugged Mrs. Bruno. Gina hugged Madame Olga. Paolo hugged Benvenuto. Then everybody hugged Luther Lewis.

"We won! We won!" shouted Paolo.

"You're a genius!" Madame Olga said to Luther, pounding him on the back. "An absolute genius!"

They left the courthouse in a flurry of excitement. Well-wishers and reporters pressed around them. Laughing and shaking hands, they pushed their way through the crowd. Finally they reached the station wagon. And the drive home was a joyous one.

That afternoon the house was filled with visitors. It seemed to Paolo as if the whole neighborhood was there. Everyone talked about the case, and patted Benvenuto, and congratulated them again and again.

It wasn't until supper time that things quieted down, and the family could relax at last.

Gina lay on the living room rug, playing with Benvenuto. She rolled over and looked up at the ceiling.

"Papa," she asked, "how old do I have to be before I can vote?"

"Eighteen," said Mr. Bruno.

Gina counted on her fingers. "That means I have nine more years to wait."

"Why do you ask, *cara?*"

"When I'm eighteen," Gina replied dreamily, "I'm going to vote for Luther Lewis for President."

CHAPTER 13
A WINTER OF CHANGES

In New York City, popularity and fame come quickly. And they just as quickly fade away. Today's hero often becomes tomorrow's forgotten man. Perhaps it's because new and unusual things are always happening in New York. A person (or a dragon) may hold the spotlight for a little while—then the spotlight moves on to some new excitement.

So it wasn't surprising that interest in Benvenuto faded rather rapidly. Of course the newspapers all carried follow-up stories. Howard B. Stokely talked about Judge

Osgood's decision on his TV show. Some of the comics on television told a lot of dragon jokes. And one chain of hamburger stands tried to promote a 50-cent "dragonburger" (which didn't sell). And that was just about that.

Letters continued to dribble in for a while. But these slowly stopped. The gifts stopped, too. This was a big relief to Gina, who had been trying to send all the givers "thank you" notes, signed with Benvenuto's paw print.

In all, the "Benvenuto Defense Fund" had collected $172.65. The Brunos offered this money to Luther Lewis as payment for his services. But Luther wouldn't take a cent.

"Absolutely not," he said. "The Benvenuto case was strictly a labor of love."

"Then what do we do with the money?" Paolo asked. "Buy $172.65 worth of dog food?!!"

The family held a conference. And it was finally decided to send the funds to Dr. Philip O'Hara as a contribution to the A.S.P.C.A.

With that out of the way, everything quieted down. And before long, life for the Brunos was back to normal.

The weeks and months went by in a pleasant routine. Every day Mr. Bruno went off to work. The children went off to school. Mrs. Bruno cooked huge meals and took care of her household.

But as time went on, certain changes took place in Benvenuto. Changes which gave Mr. Bruno a lot to think about.

For one thing, Benvenuto suddenly began to grow. By the middle of winter, he was almost four feet in length. And a lot heavier. He became so big and bulky that everyone felt cramped in the little apartment.

The dragon had long since outgrown his cardboard carton. Now, when he dozed next to Paolo's cot, his tail poked out into the living room. People kept tripping. And Mrs. Bruno had a terrible time trying to work around him with the mop and the vacuum cleaner.

Mr. Bruno noticed something else. Benvenuto was becoming an excellent hunter. The Brunos lived in a very old apartment house. Like most old buildings, it had its share of mice and roaches. Benvenuto became quite good at catching these creatures. Whenever he saw a mouse or a roach, his tail would quiver. His eyes would gleam. He would pounce as quick as a flash—and that would be the end of the invader.

When Mr. Bruno noticed this new talent of Benvenuto's, he scratched his chin thoughtfully. He also saw that Paolo and Gina were very busy with friends and schoolwork. They had little time to spare for their pet. On most days, just as she had expected, Mrs. Bruno wound up walking him . . . and grumbling.

As the months wore on, Benvenuto spent more and more time at the window. He would stand on his hind legs with his front paws on the sill, and gaze out into the street. He did this day after day, with a sad but yearning look in his eyes.

Seeing all this, it was easy enough for Mr. Bruno to put two and two together.

"Benvenuto isn't happy here any more," he said quietly. "He wants to be outside all the time. He wants his freedom."

"But this is his *home*," Paolo said.

"No," said Mr. Bruno, "the *woods* are his real home. Listen to me. When he was a baby, he needed us. He needed to be nursed and taken care of, because he was small and helpless. But he's not small and helpless any more. Not one bit. He can take care of himself now. He knows how to hunt. He knows how to move fast. And he's getting to be one very strong dragon."

Paolo and Gina tried not to hear what their father was saying. They tried hard to ignore it. But toward the end of that winter a new crisis arose. Benvenuto began to lose interest in food. He barely picked at even the tastiest morsels. With dull eyes, he would take a few listless bites and then walk away.

And finally he even turned up his nose at Mrs. Bruno's ravioli.

"He's just sick, that's all," insisted Gina. "There's a lot of virus going around."

Mr. Bruno shook his head. "He's not sick. He's *home*sick. He's pining, *cara*. Pining for the woods. And the caves. And the mountain streams. You remember when we won our

court case. That was a great victory. *Si*. But that city lawyer—he had a point. The city isn't a good place for wild things to live. Benvenuto can't stay cooped up in this little apartment forever. He's a wild creature. His world is out there. Not here."

Paolo frowned. Gina looked unhappy. They didn't like to think about it. They didn't like to talk about it. But deep down they knew that their father was right.

The time was soon coming when Benvenuto would have to leave them. Somewhere, somehow, they would have to find him a new home. A place where he could be free.

CHAPTER 14

BENVENUTO GOES HOME

Spring came early to Bleecker Street. All at once the days turned warm and sunny. There was a fresh sparkle in the air. And tiny green buds began to show on the straggly trees growing along the curb.

Now Benvenuto spent all his time standing at the window, gazing out longingly. And whenever Paolo or Mrs. Bruno took him for a walk, they had an awful time getting him back into the house again.

"We've put it off long enough," Mr. Bruno announced. "Next Saturday, if the weather's good, we take Benvenuto out to the country."

"But *where*?" Paolo asked.

"Well, I was thinking," said Mr. Bruno. "There are lots of places where I'm sure he'd do okay. But maybe the best thing is to take him back to where you found him. Remember those big woods, just past the Fresh Air camp?"

Paolo nodded. "It's nice around there. No houses. No people. There are lots of streams. And a big lake, too. He'll have plenty of water to drink."

"Those woods are full of game and plants and berries," added Mr. Bruno, "so he won't have trouble getting food."

"Maybe he'll find his old cave, Paolo," said Gina. "Or his family. Or some other dragons to be with."

Benvenuto turned his head away from the window. He twitched his tail a few times. As if he knew what they were saying, and agreed.

Madame Olga felt badly when she heard about the new plans. But she understood.

"You can use my station wagon for the trip," she said. "I'm going to miss old Benvenuto. But you're doing the right thing. No question about it."

Early Saturday morning, Mr. Bruno went and got the station wagon. They put Benvenuto on the wide deck in back, where he had lots of room. Then Mrs. Bruno and the children climbed in. And off they went.

They rode up the West Side Highway and over the George Washington Bridge. Then Mr. Bruno took the New York Thruway to Kingston. At Kingston he turned left.

Whenever the station wagon passed any cars, the other drivers were amazed to see a large green dragon staring at them out of the back window. But outside of that, the trip was quiet and uneventful.

They drove on for several hours. Past quiet farms and rolling hills and small sleepy towns. At last they came to a big lake ringed with high mountains.

"That's our lake!" Paolo said excitedly. "We're right near camp!"

Mr. Bruno drove on for another mile or so. Then he turned off on a narrow dirt road. It was filled with holes. Weeds were growing everywhere. It was easy to tell that the road hadn't been used for a very long time.

They bumped and bounced along for a while, until the road faded away into the heavy underbrush. Nearby there was a large clearing.

"This looks like a good spot," said Mr. Bruno.

He stopped the car at the edge of the clearing and everyone climbed out. Benvenuto's eyes sparkled for the first time in weeks. His forked tongue kept darting out, and his tail wagged eagerly. Without a word, Paolo leaned over and took off the dragon's collar and leash.

Benvenuto purred. He rubbed himself against Paolo. Then he rubbed against each of the others.

"You know what?" whispered Paolo. "I think he's saying goodbye."

Gina put her arms around Benvenuto's neck and hugged hard. "Now you be careful," she said.

Benvenuto's head came up. His tongue flicked out again as if to explore his new world. He trotted quickly across the clearing. At the far side he turned and looked back for a moment at the family. Then he vanished into the bushes.

Gina cried a lot on the way home, and Mrs. Bruno sat with a comforting arm around her. Paolo sat in the front seat next to his father. He bit his lip and stared quietly out the window.

After a while he said, "Know what I'm going to do? I'm going to hang his leash and collar on the wall in my room. I'm going to put a big old nail in the wall. And I'm going to hang his leash and collar up there. Where I can look at it any time I want. And whenever I look at it, I'll remember Benvenuto."

Gina stopped crying. She wiped her nose on her sleeve.

"Know what I'm going to do?" she said. "I'm going to make a big scrapbook about Benvenuto! I'm going to paste in the Lost and Found ad. And all the stories from the papers. And all the letters we got. And on the front page I'm going to draw a big picture of Benvenuto. With green crayon!"

She became so excited about her new project that everyone cheered up. And the ride back to New York was not as gloomy as Mr. Bruno had feared.

*   *   *

Several months later the Brunos found themselves in a rented car, back on the New York Thruway. They were on their way to visit Mrs. Bruno's cousin, who lived in Syracuse.

Once again they turned off at Kingston and drove through the rolling countryside. They fell silent, one by one. Vivid memories crowded their thoughts—memories of a very special pet with gentle blue eyes.

Soon they passed the big lake. On a sudden impulse, Mr. Bruno turned off onto the old dirt road. Without a word, they bumped and bounced along until they came to the clearing. Then Mr. Bruno parked.

Excited, Paolo and Gina walked along the edge of the clearing. They peered into the thick bushes. They called and whistled hopefully.

"Benvenuto! Benvenuto!"

But there was no response. Except for the chirping of birds, the woods were still and silent. Benvenuto was nowhere to be seen.

Mr. Bruno shook his head.

"Stopping here was a dumb idea," he muttered to Mrs. Bruno. "A big mistake. The animal's gone for good. The whole thing's over. *Finito*. All we did was get the kids stirred up."

He turned and raised his voice. "Paolo! Gina! It's no use. Let's go."

With long faces, the family headed back to the car.

Suddenly Paolo gripped Mr. Bruno's arm and pointed.

"Papa! Look!"

Across a heavily wooded valley, far off on the horizon, a large puff of blue smoke rose magically into the air. It rose higher and higher. For a long moment it hung motionless. Then, very slowly, it disappeared into the deep rich blue of the summer sky.

"It's Benvenuto!" Paolo shouted. "He's alive! He's doing okay! I'll bet he's out there right now, hunting up some lunch!"

Paolo looked up at his father. "It *is* Benvenuto. Isn't it, papa? Isn't it?"

Mr. Bruno smiled.

The smoke could have been anything. It could have come from a large rubbish fire. It could have been the exhaust of a big truck. Or it could have come from one of the factories near Walton.

"Isn't that Benvenuto?" Paolo insisted. "Isn't it, papa?"

Mr. Bruno put his arm around his son's shoulders.

"Maybe it is," he said softly.

And maybe it was.